Captain Hook, That's Me

Captain Hook, That's Me

By Ada B. Litchfield
Illustrations by Sonia O. Lisker

Walker and Company
New York

Library of Congress Cataloging in Publication Data

Litchfield, Ada Bassett.
   Captain Hook, that's me.

   Summary: Third-grader Judy, who can run and skate and do lots of
things well, is afraid the children in her new school will feel sorry for
her because she has a steel hook instead of a left hand.
   [1. Physically handicapped—Fiction. 2. Moving, Household—Fiction.
3. School stories]   I. Lisker, Sonia O., ill.   II. Title.

PZ7.L697Cap   1982   [Fic]   82-2570
ISBN 0-8027-6445-2   AACR2
ISBN 0-8027-6446-0 (lib. bdg.)

First published in the United States of America in 1982
by the Walker Publishing Company, Inc.

Published simultaneously in Canada by John Wiley & Sons Canada,
Limited, Rexdale, Ontario.

   ISBN: 0-8027-6445-2 Trade
          0-8027-6446-0 Reinforced

Library of Congress Catalog Card Number: 82-70495

Printed in the United States of America

10 9 8 7 6 5 4 3 2 1

With appreciation to Louise McNamara for encouragement and understanding.

A.B.L.

With thanks to Mark Lubin for his compassion, imagination and expert help.

S.O.L.

My name is Judy Johnson. Ever since I was four years old, I have worn a hook on my left arm. I wear it because I was born without a left hand. Nobody knows why. Maybe it's because of some medicine my mother took before I was born. Whatever it was, I need my hook. I need it to help my right hand do things it couldn't do alone.

My hook holds my paper down when I write or draw. It helps me hold my book open when I read. I need it to hold the paper when I cut things out, to keep my dish from sliding when I eat, and for lots of other things.

Some people say I'm handicapped. I suppose I am, but I don't think about it much. I'm too busy.

I'm a terrific runner. I love to run races with the other kids. I like to sing, too, and I love to read out loud or just to myself. Sometimes I watch TV or play games with my sister, Bunny, or my little brother, Stevie, or my friend, Harry, who lives next door.

I can do most of the things they can do. I can play dodgeball and hopscotch. I can roller skate and play Giant Steps and Red Light, and I can slide down the slide in the park and swing on the swings.

I'm even learning to ride a bike. It isn't easy. My friend, Harry, is helping me.

Harry is older and bigger than me. And besides that, he is a fresh kid. "Hi, Captain Hook," he'll say. I know he likes me. I call him Fatso and Bubble Head. He's my best friend.

One day a boy bigger than Harry came by the playground and started yelling:

Judy! Judy! Haw! Haw! Haw!

Here comes Judy Lobster Claw!

Harry took off after him. I don't know what he said or did, but that kid always walks away fast when he sees me coming. Harry won't let anyone else call me names.

Yesterday I fell off the bike twice, but on the third try I stayed on and went all the way up the driveway.

"You're a good sport, Hook Hand," Harry said.

"Of course I am, Dummy," I said right back, "but thanks anyway."

I *am* a good sport. I don't want other kids feeling sorry for me. All my friends at school are used to me now. Nobody stares at my hook anymore.

Do I mind not having a real hand on my left arm? Yes, I do. Having a hook is a pain in the neck. My mother has to help me with it every morning. The straps and buckles have to be fastened just right or the hook won't work.

I hate not being able to swing across the parallel bars at school and I hate not being able to do cartwheels like other kids. But the thing I hate most is not being able to play the piano.

Bunny knows how I feel. Sometimes when she practices, she lets me sit beside her and plunk out a little song with my right hand. She plays the other part. Then we get up and take some bows. That's what the kids do who play duets in Bunny's recitals. It's fun. But I would need two good hands to play real music. I've always wanted to play like Bunny. I wanted to so much, I used to dream about it over and over again. Then one day something happened, and I didn't dream any more piano dreams.

My father came home one night and told us he had a new job. He said we would have to move to another town. He looked happy when he said it. I guess he didn't think how the rest of us might feel.

My mother looked worried. Stevie did, too. Bunny always liked new places and meeting new people. She always wanted to go to a new school. She got so excited she spilled her milk all over the table.

I used my hook to keep my milk from spilling and set my glass down very carefully. Then I ran to my room.

I punched my pillow. How dare my father move us just like that! Why should I have to go to a new school with new kids? They would stare at my hook and maybe even make fun of me. I couldn't stand all those kids looking and pretending not to.

Stevie poked his head in my door. "Isn't it time for our story, Judy?" he asked.

"Get out of here!" I yelled. I snatched the book out of his hand and threw it on the floor. The cover flew off. Stevie backed out of the room with his mouth open.

I picked up my Raggedy Ann doll, my Snoopy Dog, my crayons and drawing paper—everything I could get my hands on. I flung them against the door, the walls, my closet, the bed—everywhere. Then I threw myself onto the bed and cried.

When my Mom came into my room a few minutes later, I thought it was Stevie again. Without looking, I sat up and threw a pillow.

"Judy!" she said. Her voice was cross. My mother is a pretty special person. But she gets angry if she catches me feeling sorry for myself.

Almost every day she tells me how someday, when my right hand is as big as it's ever going to be, I will have a left hand that looks like a real hand. It will be made of metal and plastic. It will have little motors that pick up signals from my muscles. My muscles will tell it what to do.

"How many hooks from now?" I always ask.

"Quite a few," she says. "You'll need a new hook each time you grow bigger."

Sometimes she'll say, "Judy, my beautiful, big girl, try to be patient." And she'll give me a hug.

But right now, Mom was furious. I couldn't go out to play until I told Stevie I was sorry and taped the cover back on his book. Besides that, I had to read as many stories as he wanted to hear. And he wanted to hear a lot of them.

I hated to say goodbye to Harry, "Buck up, Buckaroo," he said. "If any strange kid is mean to you, hit 'em with your hook."

"I will, Bubble Head," I said. "You can count on me." We both laughed, but I didn't feel like fun. I don't think Harry did either.

By September, we were living in our new house and it was the first day at a new school for me. My mother had already talked with my teacher. But she went with me to school anyway.

We stood by the fence waiting for the bell to ring. A girl in a plaid jacket came over to me. I thought she was going to ask me to play. But when she saw my hook, she said "Hi" and went away.

"Don't worry, honey," my mother said, "she's just shy." I knew she was trying to keep me from feeling hurt.

I was glad when the bell rang. My teacher, Miss Morris, showed me to my desk. My mother went home.

I did everything the other kids did. But I kept thinking about my old school and Harry. I felt so lonesome.

Miss Morris stayed in with me at recess. We talked about what I had done in my other school. I think she knew I wasn't ready to go out with the other kids yet.

At lunch time, I sat beside the girl in the plaid jacket. "My name is Tina," she said. She buttered my roll for me, but she didn't need to. I was glad Tina and the other kids didn't stare at me when I held down my plate with the prongs of my hook. And nobody watched me use my hook to steady my milk, either. Maybe Miss Morris had told them not to.

After lunch I played hopscotch with Tina and another girl. Tina giggled a lot. She asked me a riddle and I asked her one. Maybe this school isn't so bad after all.

"We have a surprise today," Miss Morris said when we were all back in our seats. Then she pushed some boxes out of the closet and started handing out rhythm band instruments. But Miss Morris didn't give me anything. I was so disappointed.

I bit my lip so I wouldn't cry. "Scratch that stuff, Captain Hook," Harry would have said. "Pirates don't cry."

But why was Miss Morris leaving me out? Didn't she know I was in the rhythm band back in my other school? Didn't she think I could hang a triangle on my hook and hit it with a stick in my other hand? The boxes were empty now and there was nothing for me. Nothing. This is a stupid, dumb school anyhow, I told myself.

The boy next to me kept staring. I stuck my tongue out at him and turned my back.

"Now for the surprise," Miss Morris said. She pushed a big thing out from behind her desk. It had lots of wooden keys on its top.

"This is a marimba," she said. And she picked up two sticks and played a little tune. "It's brand new," she said. "Judy is brand new, too. So Judy is going to play it."

Me? I can't play that, I thought. How can I play that thing?

"The keys have letters on them," Miss Morris said. She handed me the sticks. I put one of them between the prongs of my hook. I held the other between my thumb and two fingers.

"Now," said Miss Morris, "when I say the letters, Judy, you hit the keys. You play first with your left hand and then with your right. I'll tell you each time which hand." She looked at me and smiled. "Think you can do it?"

I nodded and held my breath.

Miss Morris showed me where to start. Then she said,

"Left CCCGAA G, Right EEDD C,
Left CCCGAA G, Right EEDD C."

I did it. I played *Old MacDonald Had a Farm*.

The kids were really staring now, but they were smiling at me, too.

I couldn't believe it. It was almost like playing the piano. But I didn't need two good hands to make music on this instrument. I knew it wouldn't always be this easy. I'd have to learn where all the keys were and lots of other stuff. But I knew if I practiced, I could do it.

I was so excited. I put the sticks down carefully and ran to Miss Morris. I had to be careful not to hit her with my hook when I threw my arms around her.

"Oh thank you! Thank you!" I shouted. "Now I don't care if I can't play the piano. I can make music with both hands on this. I don't need ten fingers to play it."

"Play it again, Judy," Tina said.

Miss Morris said the notes and I went faster this time.

"Know what I think?" I said. "I think I'm going to be the best marimba player in the whole world."

"Of course you are," said Miss Morris. "Why not!"